Runtime

written & illustrated by
Jasmine Patel

PUZZLE PIECE  PUBLISHING

Dedicated to my fun family, my wonderful teachers, and JB who named his senior project after me.

Runtime
Story & Illustrations Copyright © 2019 by Jasmine Patel

a b c d e f g h i j k l m n o p q r s t u v w x y z
Penguin Typeface Copyright © 2019 by Genevieve Johnson

First hardcover edition August 2020

Isbn: 978-1-7355952-0-7 (hardcover)
Isbn: 978-1-7355952-1-4 (ebook)

Puzzle Piece Publishing

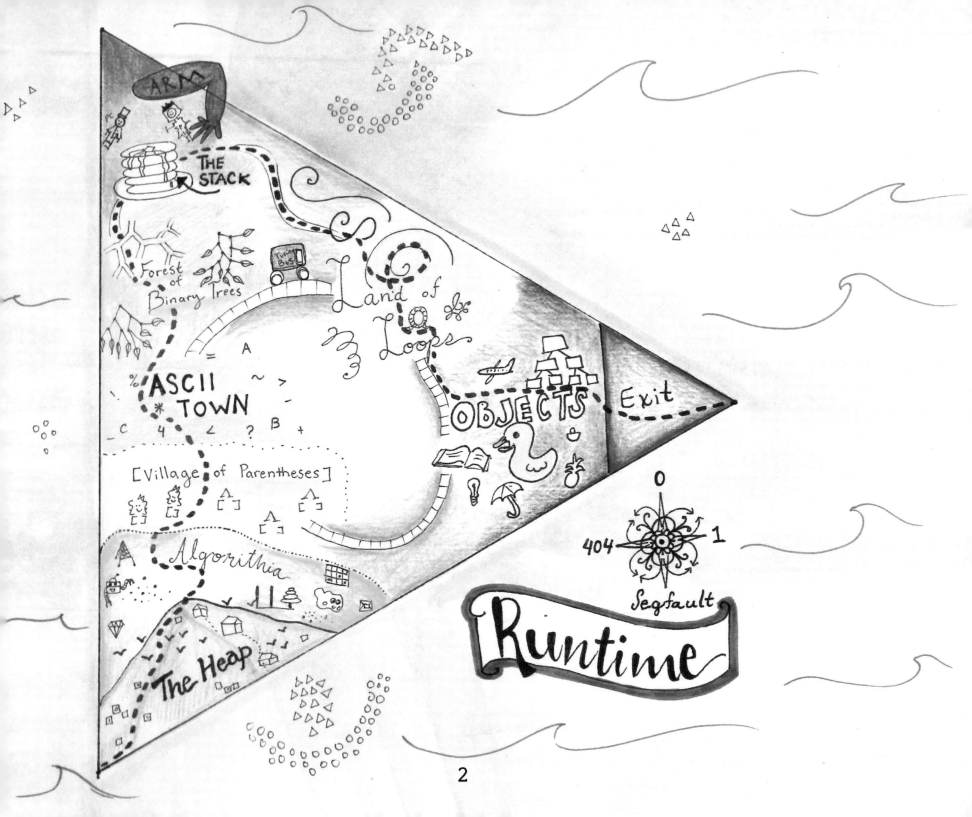

This is Charlie. She is the main character.

We can call her "Char."

Today is Char's birthday! She got lots of exciting gifts. She even got a brand new computer!

Char soon realized the computer was very boring.

It doesn't do anything!

She decided to press a key...

Char opened the note. Then she read from the note.

Dear Char,

Welcome to Runtime. Help us find bugs! To return home, find some traveling objects!

Lucky bugs look like this and appear on every page.

Unlucky bugs look like this and appear only on some pages.

A semicolon looks like this.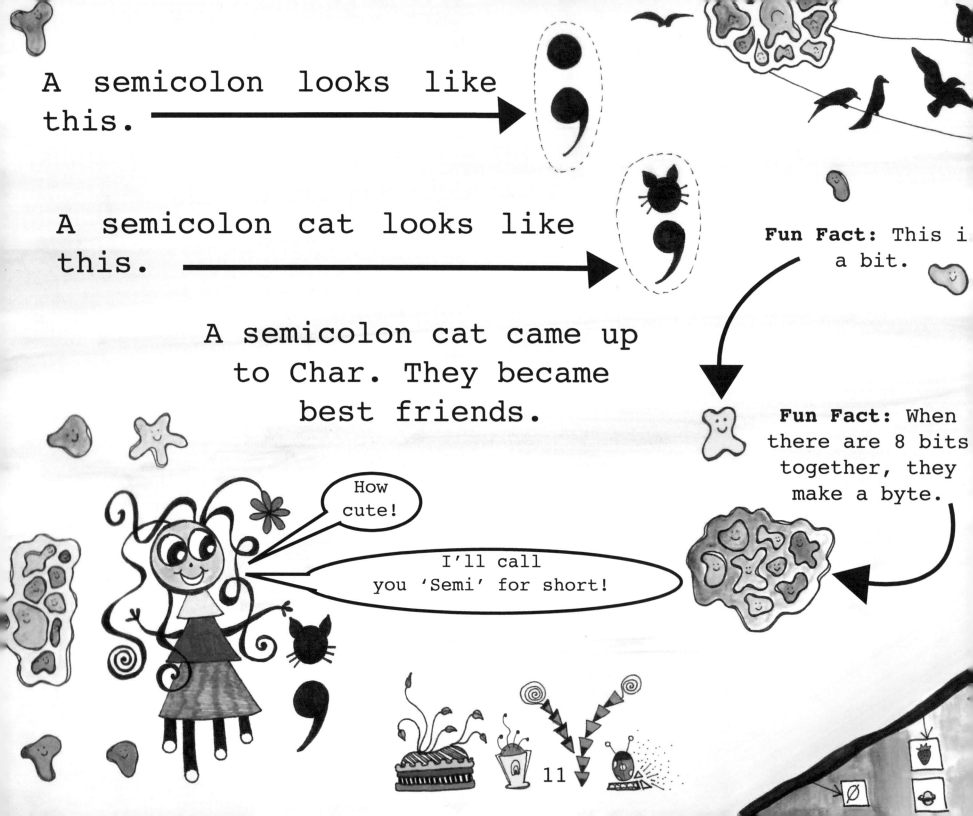

A semicolon cat looks like this.

A semicolon cat came up to Char. They became best friends.

How cute!

I'll call you 'Semi' for short!

Fun Fact: This i
a bit.

Fun Fact: When there are 8 bits together, they make a byte.

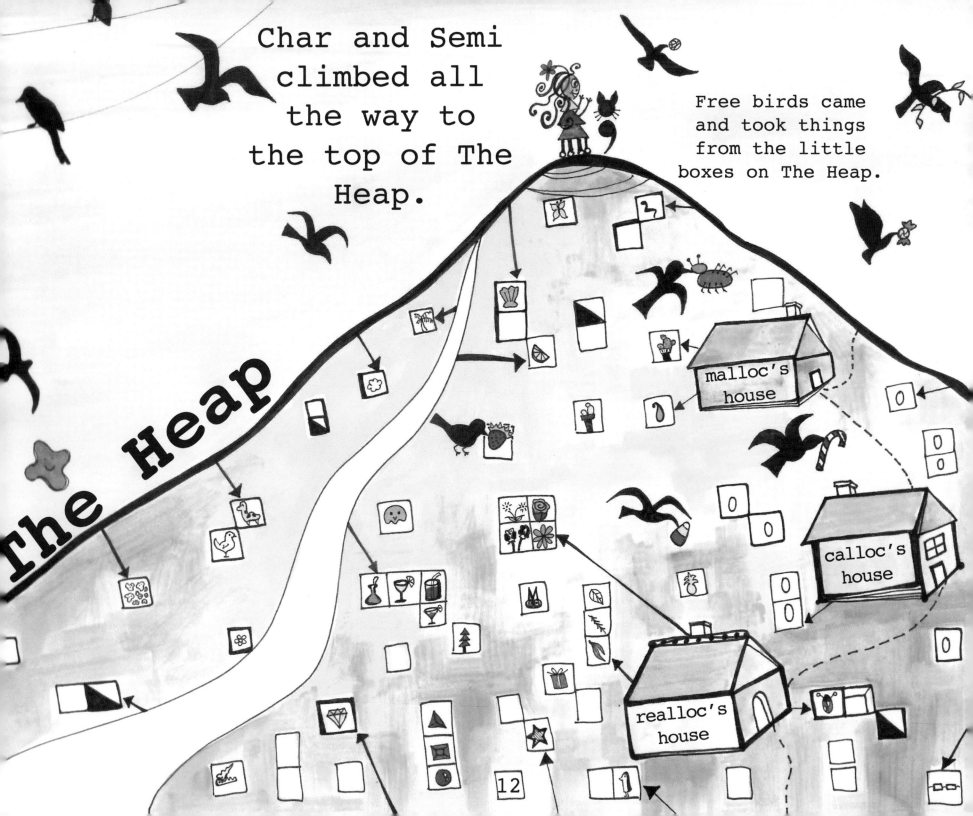

Char and Semi climbed all the way to the top of The Heap.

Free birds came and took things from the little boxes on The Heap.

The Heap

malloc's house

calloc's house

realloc's house

0

0

0

0

0

0

0

0

0

0

12

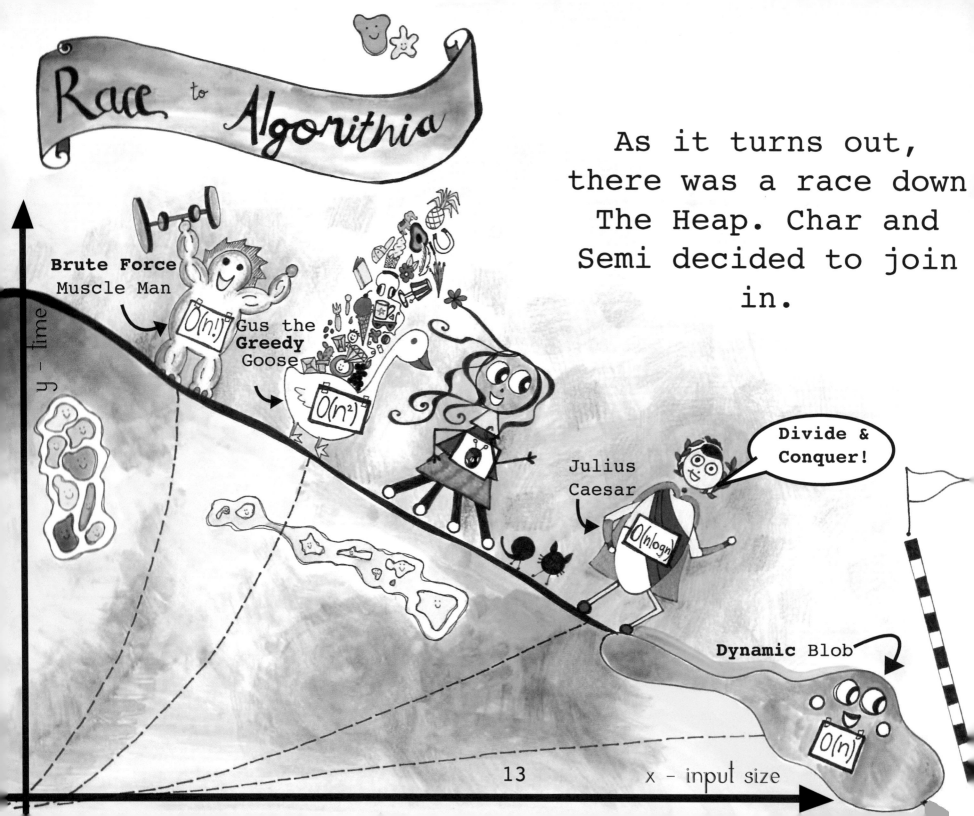

Cell Tower Placing

Welcome to **ALGORITHIA**

Max Dropping Distance

Towers of Hanoi

There were lots of cool puzzles to solve in the Land of Algorithia!

Knapsack

Char and Semi decided to follow the green road to a Village.

obot Coin

Robot Cookie

Can you find the two closest dots?

14

Village of Parentheses

Opening Parenthesis

Closing Parenthesis

Opening Square Bracket

Closing Square Bracket

Closing Curly Bracket

Opening Curly Bracket

15

All opening parentheses need matching closing parentheses. Help us match things up!

Everything is all matched up!

17

ASCII TOWN

Char and Semi wandered into ASCII Town.

Char recognized some of the characters, but a lot of them were new friends!

In all of the commotion,
Semi went missing!

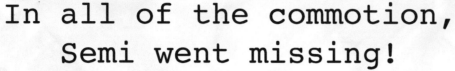

Char found a clue
to help her find
Semi, but she could
not understand it.

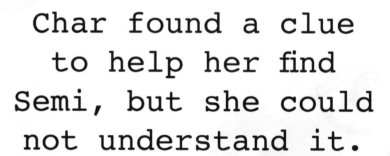

Clue:

```
01000110 01001111 01010010
01000101 01010011 01010100
```

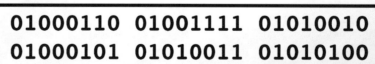

19

The Wise Interpreter came and explained what the clue meant.

The clue is written in Binary and spells the word "FOREST."
You should go to the Binary Forest!

F 01000110

O 01001111

R 01010010

E 01000101

S 01010011

T 01010100

Clue:

01000110 01001111 01010010
01000101 01010011 01010100

binary forest this way–>

Char went through a pipe to the Binary Forest.

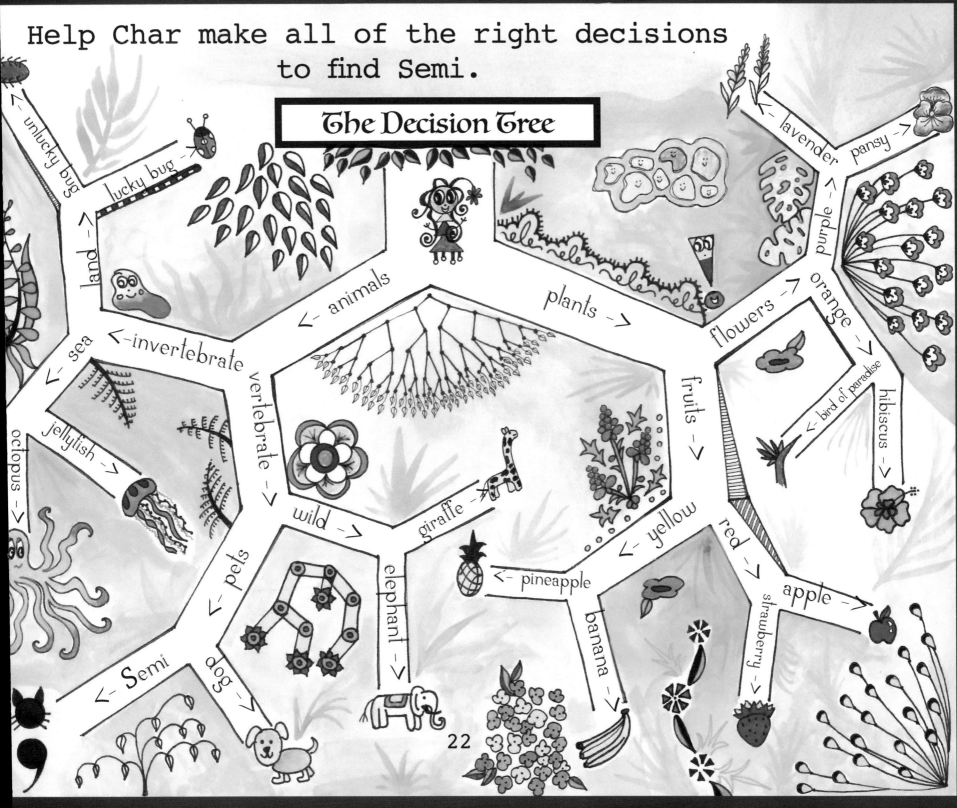

Help Char make all of the right decisions to find Semi.

The Decision Tree

22

hat does it mean to be a stack?

LIFO: The Last In is the First Out.

You can only add pancakes to the top of the stack.

You can only take pancakes from the top of the stack.

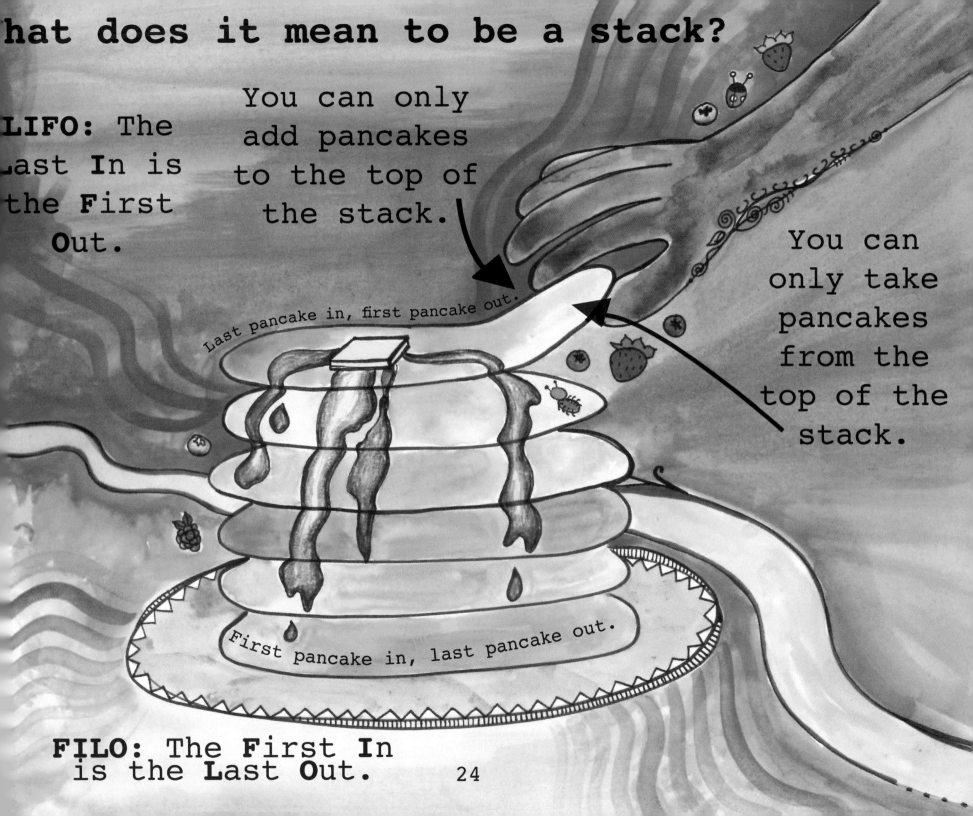

Last pancake in, first pancake out.

First pancake in, last pancake out.

FILO: The First In is the Last Out.

While Semi led the way, they headed to the Land of Loops. For each flower that they passed, if one of the petals was gold, Char picked it.

nested loops

Land of Loops →

This is a UML diagram. It gets more specific as you go down the chart.

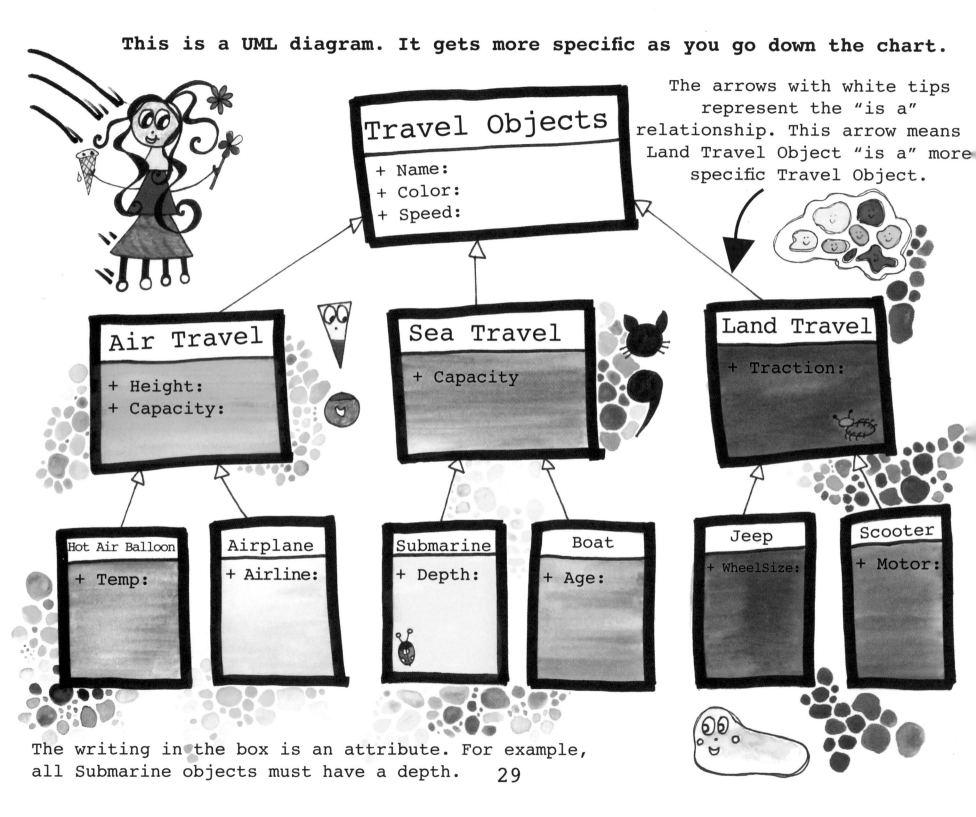

The arrows with white tips represent the "is a" relationship. This arrow means Land Travel Object "is a" more specific Travel Object.

Travel Objects

+ Name:
+ Color:
+ Speed:

Air Travel

+ Height:
+ Capacity:

Sea Travel

+ Capacity

Land Travel

+ Traction:

Hot Air Balloon

+ Temp:

Airplane

+ Airline:

Submarine

+ Depth:

Boat

+ Age:

Jeep

+ WheelSize:

Scooter

+ Motor:

The writing in the box is an attribute. For example, all Submarine objects must have a depth.   29

Which one should Char choose?

Name: Osten
Color: Yellow
Speed: 11 MPH
Capacity: 20 p
Depth: 1999 In

Name: MOt
Color: Blue
Speed: 8 MPH
Height: 1969 Ft
Capacity: 4 p
Temp: 711 F

Name: ARO
Color: Pink
Speed: 85 MPH
Traction: Medium
Motor: No

Name: Pablo
Color: Green
Speed: 711 MPH
Height: 54,000 Ft
Capacity: 1965 p
Airline: 808 Air

Name: Jbier
Color: Red
Speed: 404 MPH
Traction: Good
WheelSize: 11 In

Name: Ki Ki D
Color: Orange
Speed: 3 MPH
Capacity: 8 p
Age: 2001 y

Char returned home.

exit(0)

The 0 means there were no errors in Runtime.

31

What does it all mean?

Let's start at the beginning...

Runtime ~ *The title of this book* ~ Runtime refers to the time it takes for a computer program to be run. When things happen while a program is running, you can say they happen "in Runtime."

The Map (pg. 2) ~ *The fantasy map is in the shape of a triangular play button* ~ In some coding editors, you need to press the play button to enter Runtime. The Stack is on the top, and the Heap is on the bottom. This is true in most computer memory layouts. There are little clusters of islands around the main Runtime Island. These represent famous datasets used to measure accuracy of clustering algorithms.

Char (pg. 4) ~ *The main character* ~ In computer science, a Char is a datatype used to represent one character. For example, 'a' is a char.

Most of the words in the story are written in the font `Courier New` ~ This is a common font used for coding because it is monospaced. That means each character takes up the same amount of horizontal space.

The Shell (pg. 7) ~ *A magical shell appears when Char presses a key on her computer* ~ In computer science, the shell is something you can type commands into. The shell is used for communication between the user (the person using the computer) and the operating system (the inside of the computer).

HASH BANG SLASH BIN SLASH BASH (pg. 7) ~ *When The Shell appears, it makes some noises* ~ Hash is the name of the "#" symbol. Bang is the name of the "!" symbol. Slash is the name of the "/" symbol. These noisy words actually translate to "#!/bin/bash" which is a line of code that you should always include when writing a bash shell script.

README (pg. 9) ~ *After Char falls in The Shell, she sees a note that says "README"* ~ In computer science, most well written programs have a file called "README," which contains important information about how the program works and how to use it properly. It is always a good idea to read the README file before working on an existing program.

Char opens the note. Then she reads from the note (pg. 10) ~ These are two separate steps because in many coding languages reading a file requires two steps: opening and reading.

Lucky Bugs (pg. 10) ~ *Char is tasked with finding Lucky Bugs on every page* ~ In computer science, a bug is a problem with your code. Programmers spend most of their time finding bugs and fixing them. Lucky bugs appear every time a program is run, so they are easier to track down.

Unlucky Bugs (pg. 10) ~ *Char is also tasked with finding Unlucky Bugs* ~ However, they only appear on some pages. In computer science, an unlucky bug is a bug that is difficult to find because it does not always appear every time a program is run. If you do not locate an unlucky bug on a page, it does not mean that one is not there. Perhaps you just cannot find it. On the other hand, there might not be a bug at all, and you are just wasting your time. Frustrating, right?

Semicolon Cat (pg. 11) ~ *A semicolon cat, Semi, becomes best friends with Char* ~ Many coding languages require programmers to type a semicolon at the end of every line of code. Programmer tend to spend a lot of time with semicolons.

Bits & Bytes (pg. 11) ~ *There are tiny bits floating around* ~ Eight bits together are a byte. I computer science, a bit is the tiniest unit of data. It can either be a 1 or a 0. When there are 8 bit it equals 1 byte. This is similar to how 10 millimeters equals 1 centimeter.

The Heap (pg. 12) ~ *Char and Semi climb up the mountain called The Heap* ~ In compute science, the heap is memory storage for use during runtime (along with The Stack, which w will get to later). Char notices lots of little boxes with things in them scattered throughout Th Heap in no particular order. These represent the storage spaces. In the story, malloc, calloc, an realloc each have houses on the heap. In computer science, malloc, calloc, and realloc are cal you can make to allocate memory, basically to reserve some space. Malloc is short for "Memor Allocation." The 'C' in Calloc stands for 'clear' because calloc always fills memory with 0's. Yo can use realloc to change the size of your existing storage space. The arrows are pointers tha keep track of boxes.

Free Birds (pg. 12) ~ *There are free birds that take things off of The Heap* ~ In computer science it is important to always call "free" when you are finished with the memory you allocated. Th keeps everything nice and clean. It is just like putting away toys when you are done playing wit them.

The Race to Algorithia (pg. 13) ~ *Char and Semi join in a race* ~ In computer science, programme are always trying to find the fastest way to solve problems. The characters that they race again each symbolize a different method of solving problems. Brute Force, Greedy, Divide & Conque and Dynamic Programming are all common ways to solve challenging coding problems. The speeds vary from problem to problem, but in general they finish in about the order depicted o page 13. The race tags, which are written in Big-O notation, represent their speed. The dotte lines that connect them to the bottom left corner symbolize a typical time vs. size graph.

Algorithia (pg. 14) ~ *There were lots of cool puzzles to solve in the land of Algorithia* ~ The land is based on famous computer science problems and the algorithms used to solve them.

Towers of Hanoi (pg. 14) ~ The goal in this puzzle is to move the stack of rings from the rod on the right to the rod on the left. This must be done by moving one ring at a time and never stacking a larger ring on top of a smaller ring.

Robot Coin (pg. 14) ~ The goal of this puzzle is to tell the robot which squares to visit so that it can pick up the most coins (since not every square contains a coin). The tricky part is that the robot cannot visit two squares that are next to each other.

Robot Cookie (pg. 14) ~ This puzzle is similar to the Robot Coin puzzle, except it is two-dimensional. The goal is to find which squares the robot should visit to pick up the most cookies. Not every square has a cookie on it (Some were eaten off the tray prior to the robot's arrival.) The robot starts at the top left square and tries to get to the bottom right square. It can only move one square at a time downward or to the right.

Knapsack (pg. 14) ~ The knapsack problem is a famous algorithm problem in which a student needs to choose which items to put into the knapsack so that he or she can maximize its value. Each item has a different weight and value and the knapsack is limited in size. There are different strategies that can be utilized to accomplish this.

Can you find the two closest dots? (pg. 14) ~ This is one of my favorite algorithm puzzles. The algorithm is complicated and typically a "Divide & Conquer" approach works best. However, when the set is fairly small and the differences are not too slight, the human eye can easily identify the two closest dots. It is one of those examples where humans are faster than computers.

Max Dropping Distance (pg. 14) ~ The premise of this puzzle is to find the highest rung of a ladder from which you can drop a camera without breaking it. One way to do that is to start at the bottom rung and drop the camera. If it does not break, then try from the next rung. You can keep moving up the ladder one rung at a time until it breaks. Then you will know the one before that was the max dropping distance. However this can take a lot of time. There are easier ways to do this without using too many cameras!

Cell Tower Placing (pg. 14) ~ There are many variations of this problem, but the basic idea is that you have a road and a bunch of houses along the road. You need to find the best spots to place the cell towers so that each house is close to at least one cell tower. There are a limited number of cell towers and you want to use as few as possible.

Village of Parentheses (pg. 15) ~ *Char and Semi visit the Village of Parentheses* ~ In computer science, parentheses are *very, very, very* important. Square brackets, curly brackets, and parentheses each have their own special use which vary from coding language to coding language. In general, parentheses need to be matched up. If there is an opening one without a closing one (or vice versa), it causes many bugs which can often be hard to find. The matching activity is designed to emphasize this point.

ASCII* Town (pg. 18) ~ *Char and Semi visit ASCII Town* ~ Yay! We are finally here! You may be familiar with the 26 character English alphabet. The ASCII alphabet is similar except it has 256 characters. Basically every symbol on your keyboard is a character. This includes all of the lowercase letters, all of the capital letters, all of the numbers, and all of the symbols. Even the empty symbol, which appears when you press the space bar, is part of the ASCII alphabet! In computer science, the char data type refers to one single ASCII character. This is why each ASCII character in ASCII Town has the same colors as Char. They are all chars!

*ASCII (/æski/) stands for American Standard Code for Information Interchange. ASCII tables are used and known by most computer scientists.

Semi goes missing (pg. 19) ~ I could not resist this pun opportunity. One of the most common problems that computer scientists face is that they are missing a semicolon in their code. This can be extremely difficult to track down and will cause many bugs and unexpected program behavior. Computer scientists worldwide have had many sleepless nights due to missing semicolons.

The Clue (pg. 19) ~ *Char finds a clue to help her find Semi* ~ Binary is a language made out of bits. If you remember from earlier, a bit is either a 1 or a 0. If you have a byte (8 bits) and each one can either be a 1 or a 0, you have 256 different combinations of 1's and 0's. These map directly to the 256 ASCII characters. If you look them up in an ASCII table, you can tell which bytes map to which characters and crack the code!

The Interpreter (pg. 20) ~ *The interpreter translates the clue* ~ This page is Programming Language (PL) themed. In certain PL's, there is an interpreter which executes instructions. On the right side of the page, there are symbols. Each one is based on a coding language. In order from top to bottom, they are: Java, Python, C, Ruby, Perl, C++.

The Pipe (pg. 20) ~ *Char goes through a pipe to reach the Binary Forest* ~ In computer science, different processes can communicate with each other using pipes. Pipes are used to pass information back and forth.

The Dining Philosophers (pg. 21) ~ *Char comes across some dining philosophers in the forest* ~ In computer science, "the dining philosophers" is a famous operating system (OS) problem. The philosophers symbolize different processes. The processes need resources, such as space and time, similar to the way the philosophers need a fork and knife. Occasionally if each process has some resources but not enough to complete, then they can get stuck. The solution to this is to take turns!

The Philosophers (pg. 21) ~ I based each of the philosophers after an actual philosopher in history. Starting from the left, the first one is Aristotle, who is famous for logic. The next one is Confucius, who is known for quotes about how to live a good life. The next is Descartes. He is pictured with a fly. At one point in his life, he was watching a fly, which made him come up with the Cartesian plane concept that is widely used today. The last one is Newton, who is pictured watching an apple drop. He is famous for discovering gravity while watching an apple from a tree.

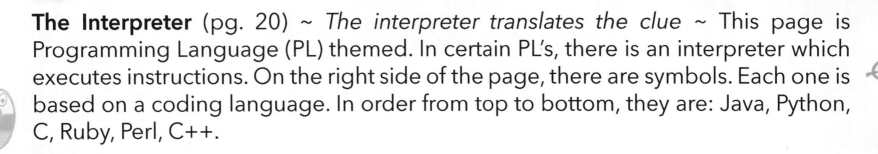

The Decision Tree (pg. 22) ~ *Char uses a decision tree to help her find Semi* ~ In computer science, decision trees are used for classification. For example, if you had a purple flower but did not know what it was called, you could trace it down the tree, turning down the "plants" path and the "flower" path and the "purple" path. Then you could decide if it was lavender or perhaps a pansy. Decision trees help computers and robots decide what to do based on other things that have already been done.

The Stack (pg. 23) ~ *Char and Semi head to the giant stack of pancakes* ~ In computer science, a stack is many things. It is a main part of a computer memory layout. It is also a data structure. It has the FILO (first in last out) aka LIFO (last in first out) property. You can push things onto a stack and pop them off. The Program Counter (PC) controls the stack by keeping track of which instruction is currently being executed. The Stack Pointer (SP) keeps track of the top of the stack. The Pancake Chef (PC) symbolizes the PC while the Syrup Princess (SP) symbolizes the SP. It might be fun to try making a stack out of books or blocks (or pancakes, yum)!

The ARM (pg. 23) ~ *There is a giant arm next to the stack of pancakes* ~ In Computer Science, ARM is an example of an assembly language which means it is made up of simple statements that can be translated to 1's and 0's. ARM, along with other programming languages, can be used to manipulate the stack.

The Land of Loops (pg. 25) ~ *While Semi led the way, for each flower, if one of the petals…* ~ These are all examples of the way code is written. Logic is broken down into loops. The "while", "for", and "for-each" are different types of loops. The "if" statement is a conditional statement. When you have multiple loops at once, it is referred to as a nested loop.

The Queue (pg. 26) ~ *Char and Semi wait in line for the Queue* ~ In computer science, the queue is another data structure. It has the FIFO (first in first out) aka LILO (last in last out) property. It is fun to be the first person in line at a ride, but if you are last, like Char, you will probably have to wait a while.

The Traveling Salesperson (pg. 27) ~ *Char buys ice cream from the Traveling Salesperson* ~ The Traveling Salesperson, or TSP for short, is one of the hardest and most famous computer science problems. The answer to the example in the story is: Here -> The Stack -> ASCII Town -> The Heap -> Here. Or the same thing backwards: Here -> The Heap -> ASCII Town -> The Stack -> Here. This example was not too tough, but imagine if there were 1,000 places. That would take much longer to figure out!

Turing Bus (pg. 27) ~ No, not a typo. The Turing Bus is named after Alan Turing, who is known for being the Father of Computer Science. He created the Turing machine, which is the first basic computer. He was interested in testing the limits of computing. Nowadays coding languages must be "Turing complete"; that means they can do all of the basic things. The arrows and circles on the bus symbolize an abstract diagram of a Turing machine. The track symbolizes the "tape," an aspect of a Turing machine.

OBJECTS (pg. 28) ~ *Char and Semi visit the place called Objects* ~ This land is based on Object Oriented Programming (OOP). In OOP, computer scientists define data types called classes. For example, you can define a shape class. You can also give attributes to the data types. The shape class might have an attribute for color, size, and number of corners.

Rubber Duck (pg. 28) ~ *In the pile of objects, there is a rubber duck* ~ Lots of software engineers keep rubber ducks on their desks. When they are stuck writing code, it helps them to talk out loud to the duck.

UML Diagram (pg. 29) ~ *The UML diagram of travel objects is used to describe the different options of travel that Char has* ~ In computer science, UML diagrams are used to map out different classes and how they are related. The arrows with the white tips symbolize an "is a" relationship. A Scooter "is a" Land Travel Object. That means a Scooter has to have everything a Scooter needs plus everything a Land Travel Object needs. A Land Travel Object is a Travel Object so therefore it needs everything a Travel Object needs. It is confusing at first, but UML diagrams really help to get the hang of Object Oriented Programming.

Exit(0) (pg. 31) ~ *Char finally leaves Runtime* ~ Exit(0) means there were no errors and everything finished smoothly.

Return (pg. 28) ~ Char returned home. Return is a keyword used to end a function.

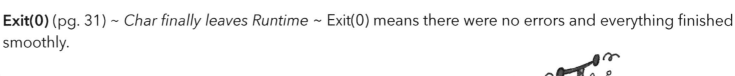

Thanks for reading!

40

CPSIA information can be obtained at www.ICGtesting.com
Printed in the USA
BVIW122352231220
595971BV00010B/75

9 781735 595207